LET'S FIND OUT! BIOMES

WHAT ARE DESERTS?

PHILIP WOLNY

Britannica Educational Publishing
IN ASSOCIATION WITH
ROSEN
EDUCATIONAL SERVICES

Published in 2019 by Britannica Educational Publishing (a trademark of Encyclopædia Britannica, Inc.) in association with The Rosen Publishing Group, Inc.
29 East 21st Street, New York, NY 10010

Distributed exclusively by Rosen Publishing.
To see additional Britannica Educational Publishing titles, go to rosenpublishing.com.

First Edition

Britannica Educational Publishing
J.E. Luebering: Executive Director, Core Editorial
Mary Rose McCudden: Editor, Britannica Student Encyclopedia

Rosen Publishing
Amelie von Zumbusch: Editor
Matt Cauli: Series Designer
Tahara Anderson: Book Layout
Cindy Reiman: Photography Manager
Nicole DiMella: Photo Researcher

Library of Congress Cataloging-in-Publication Data

Names: Wolny, Philip, author.
Title: What are deserts? / Philip Wolny.
Description: First edition. | New York : Britannica Educational Publishing, in Association with Rosen Educational Services, 2019. | Series: Let's find out! Biomes | Audience: Grades 1–5. | Includes index. | Includes bibliographical references and index.
Identifiers: LCCN 2018009223| ISBN 9781508106951 (library bound) | ISBN 9781508107095 (paperback) | ISBN 9781508107378 (6 pack)
Subjects: LCSH: Desert biology—Juvenile literature. | Deserts—Juvenile literature.
Classification: LCC QH88 .W65 2019 | DDC 578.754—dc23
LC record available at https://lccn.loc.gov/2018009223

Manufactured in the United States of America

Photo credits: Cover and interior pages background Anton Foltin/Shutterstock.com; p. 4 © Encyclopædia Britannica, Inc.; p. 5 Cat Downie/Shutterstock.com; p. 6 Vladimir Wrangel/Shutterstock.com; p. 7 Scenics of America/PhotoLink/Getty Images; p. 8 Julian Schaldach/Shutterstock.com; p. 9 JeniFoto/Shutterstock.com; p. 10 liuzishan/iStock/Thinkstock; p. 11 Scott Smith/Corbis Documentary/Getty Images; p. 12 automidori/Moment/Getty Images; p. 13 N Mrtgh/Shutterstock.com; p. 14 Gerald Cubitt/Bruce Coleman Ltd; p. 15 Danita Delimont/Gallo Images/Getty Images; p. 16 © Nicolas Durance/Fotolia; p. 17 Robert Stolting/Shutterstock.com; p. 18 © orxy/Fotolia; p. 19 © James Insogna/Fotolia.; p. 20 © Tom Algire; p. 21 Dianne Millard/U.S. National Park Service; p. 22 © David_Steele/Fotolia; p. 23 Photo Researchers/Science Source/Getty Images; p. 24 bmphotographer/Shutterstock.com; p. 25 CrackerClips Stock Media/Shutterstock.com; p. 26 © Claire.B/Fotolia; p. 27 © Crobard/Fotolia; p. 28 © Maher Najm; p. 29 Fadel Senna/AFP/Getty Images.

Contents

The Driest Biome

A biome is a large region of Earth that has a certain climate and certain types of living things. A desert is one kind of biome. Some other biomes include tundra, forests, and grasslands.

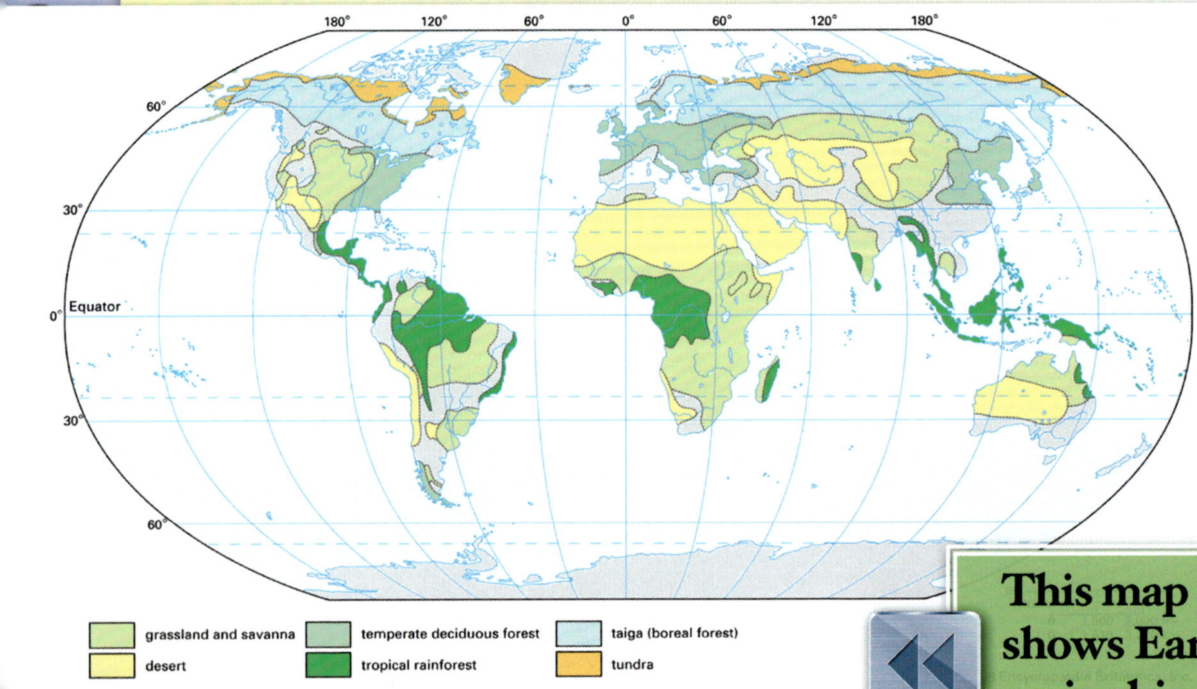

This map shows Earth's major biomes.

Think About It

What kind of traits would be helpful for animals and plants in a desert to have?

Deserts cover about 20 percent of Earth's land surface, and every continent has at least one desert. When people think of a desert, they usually think of a sandy, hot, and dry place. But there are other types of deserts as well. A desert is any large region that gets very little rain each year. This lack of water means that very few plants or animals live in desert areas. The plants and animals that live in deserts around the world have traits that help them to survive in their particular areas.

This desert fox, photographed in a desert region of Egypt, is a common animal for this environment.

Hot Deserts

There are hot, cold, and temperate deserts. The world's hottest deserts are in areas closest to the **equator**, in the region known as the tropics. This is a band of Earth on either side of the equator. The sunlight is very strong in the tropics, which makes the area warmer than other parts of Earth.

Vocabulary

The equator is an imaginary circle around Earth. It runs east and west halfway between the North and South poles.

A camel caravan travels through the Sahara in Morocco.

The world's largest hot desert is the Sahara in northern Africa. Other hot deserts include the Mojave in the southwestern United States and the Kalahari in southern Africa.

In hot deserts daytime temperatures are often above 100° Fahrenheit (38° Celsius) in summer. Al Aziziyah, Libya, experienced the hottest temperature ever recorded, at 136°F (57.8°C). Death Valley, California, has come close at 134°F (56.7°C).

Death Valley National Park is located in southeastern California.

Even in a hot desert, the temperatures can get quite cold at night. The air cools quickly after sunset. This is because the desert's air and bare earth are both dry. There are no clouds to trap heat in. The lack of clouds also means that the ground gets very hot when the sun rises. In non-desert biomes, clouds reflect much of the sunlight.

The sun burns hot over the dunes in Erg Chebbi, part of the Moroccan Sahara.

Some hot deserts have huge temperature differences depending on time of day. The temperatures can be 40° F (21.4° C) hotter during the day than at night.

The temperature of the soil surface can rise even higher than the air temperature. Soil surface temperatures as high as 172°F (78°C) have been recorded in the Sahara.

Compare and Contrast

Think about how much rain you get in the biome you live in. Compare and contrast the climate you are used to with the one in a hot desert.

The setting sun colors these desert mountains outside of Phoenix, Arizona, a rich red. This area is part of the Sonoran Desert.

COLD AND TEMPERATE DESERTS

Antarctica, the ice-covered land around the South Pole, is considered a cold desert. It gets very little precipitation, but the main reason that few things live there is the cold temperatures.

Temperate deserts are found between the polar

This image from China's Xinjiang region shows a section of the Gobi, a temperate desert.

regions and the tropics, in the middle latitudes. They occur mainly in Central Asia. There are also smaller areas in western North America, southeastern South America, and Australia. These deserts are often separated from the coast by mountains or by great distance. Air picks up moisture from the ocean, but by the time it reaches these regions, it has lost much of its moisture.

The Black Rock Desert, in Nevada, is surrounded by several mountain ranges.

> **VOCABULARY**
>
> **Plateaus are raised, high, flat areas, often surrounded on one or more sides by mountains, cliffs, or steep slopes.**

Many temperate deserts exist in places that are high above sea level. This includes high places between mountain ranges, called **plateaus**.

Temperate deserts get most of their precipitation during the colder months. The precipitation can be in the form of rain or snow. They have hot summers and cold winters.

The biggest temperate desert is the Gobi in Central Asia. The biggest temperate desert in the United States is the Great Basin Desert, which covers nearly all of Nevada, western Utah, and portions

The Kumtag Desert in northwestern China is shown here with some snow cover during winter.

Some areas of the Great Basin experience their share of cold weather.

of surrounding states. It includes the Great Sandy Desert of southeastern Oregon, the Snake River Plains of southern Idaho, the volcanic Black Rock Desert of northwestern Nevada, and the Great Salt Lake Desert of western Utah.

Think About It

In some deserts, when they do get precipitation they may get a lot at once. What do you think the effects of getting rare but heavy precipitation might be?

Coastal Deserts

Most coastal deserts lie on the western coasts of South America and Africa. The winds in these areas tend to blow in such ways that they keep clouds with rain away from the land. Cold ocean currents also keep the air dry. The Namib Desert in southwestern Africa is one example of a coastal desert. Another is the Atacama Desert

The Namib, a coastal desert in southern Africa, is shown here with plant life blooming.

in South America. The parts of coastal deserts that are closest to the water are warm but not hot during the summers and cool in winter. Further inland the deserts may be hotter.

Water in coastal deserts comes mostly in the form of fog. Fog forms over the nearby oceans and then drifts over the deserts. Some water droplets condense on the leaves of plants, or even on the rocks or soil.

VOCABULARY

Fog is tiny water drops hovering in the air. It is like a cloud, but it is near the ground.

The Atacama Desert meets the Pacific Ocean in this stretch of Chile's Pan de Azúcar National Park.

LANDFORMS

Deserts differ greatly in their land features. They may include dunes of shifting sand, mountains, bare rock, or plains of gravel and boulders. Sand dunes are not as common in deserts as many people think. For example, they make up only about 10 percent of the Sahara of northern Africa.

A common type of desert consists of mountains separated by basins called bolsons. The mountains receive most of the rains in downpours.

These huge sand dunes can be found in Abu Dhabi, the United Arab Emirates, much of which lies within the Arabian Desert.

Vocabulary

When water **evaporates**, it seems to disappear. When water is warmed by heat, it changes from a liquid state (regular water) to a gas that becomes part of the air, known as water vapor.

As the water rushes down the steep slopes it cuts deep gullies.

Sometimes floodwaters make temporary shallow lake in basins. The lakes that form in basins with no outlet are called playa lakes. Typically the water **evaporates** or drains away, leaving behind sediments. The flat-bottomed depression that is formed is called a playa.

The light area in front of these mountains is part of the playa of the Black Rock Desert, in Nevada.

Desert Plants

Desert plants have features that help them survive in the dry climate. Different plants have different ways of surviving. Some depend upon underground water and have long root systems. Other plants can absorb water droplets in the air.

Ordinary non-desert plants take up water from the soil by means of their roots and give off water

This unusual plant, the tumboa (*Welwitschia mirabilis*), lives in deserts in southwestern Africa. Some of these plants live to be more than a thousand years old.

Think About It

Some desert plants do not grow in any other part of the world. Why do you think that is?

through their leaves. This process is called transpiration. Some desert plants, such as the cactus, have no leaves or only very small ones that usually drop off as the plant matures. They thus avoid a huge loss of water.

Cacti are succulent plants. This means that they have thick tissues that take up and hold large amounts of water. The stored water keeps them alive during dry periods.

The saguaro cactus is native to the Sonoran Desert, which is in northern Mexico and the southwestern United States.

Another succulent that lives in deserts is the yucca. These members of the agave plant family grow in North America. Yuccas store water in their thick, waxy leaves.

Some desert plants survive by having unusual life cycles. Certain plants sprout when the rain falls, bloom quickly, ripen their seed in a few days, and then wither and die. Others survive a lack of water by drying up, just for a time. When water comes back, they go back to normal.

Some plants live in balance with their neighbors

Yucca plants grow in the sand of White Sands National Monument in New Mexico.

COMPARE AND CONTRAST

How are yuccas and cacti similar? In what ways are they different?

by growing quite far apart. This way, there is more water to go around. Trees and large shrubs can be found in some deserts, but there are not many of them in the driest ones.

People rarely associate flowers with deserts, but plenty of desert plants bloom at some point during the year.

Desert Animals

Animals live in all but the toughest desert environments. Desert animals have special characteristics, or traits, that help them survive in their surroundings. They have developed these traits through a process called **adaptation**.

Camels are very well adapted to living in deserts. These are Arabian camels, also known as dromedaries.

Vocabulary

Adaptation is the process by which species change over time to better survive where they live.

For example, camels have adapted over many thousands of years to be able to go for long periods of time without drinking water. Most desert animals, including birds and insects, get the majority of their water from their food.

To save water and energy, animals might not move around much when it is hot or when water is low. They may hide from the sun during the hottest hours of the day and come out at night to feed. More than half of desert animals live at least part of the time underground, where it is cooler. Some animals, such as birds, move around to areas where it recently rained.

Native to North America, burrowing owls use the abandoned underground homes of other animals for shelter.

Many unique animals live in deserts. For example, Australia's deserts have many kinds of reptiles that are not found anywhere else. Other kinds of animals, such as kangaroos, live there, too.

In the hot deserts of Africa and Asia, many of the larger animals are domesticated. Domestic animals are ones that have been tamed for use by humans. These include camels, donkeys, goats, sheep, and horses. Wild species such as gazelles, ibexes, and oryxes are rarer. Smaller animals, including rodents that burrow into the ground and reptiles like

The thorny devil lizard lives in the Australian Outback, a vast, dry area in the interior of the country.

THINK ABOUT IT

What is an advantage of being a smaller creature in the desert when it comes to getting food and water?

snakes and lizards, are more common.

Insects and spiders are common in deserts everywhere. Spiders, beetles, centipedes, moths, butterflies, ants, dragonflies and other bugs feed off plants and other small creatures. They also provide a food and water source for larger animals.

This tarantula lives in California's Joshua Tree National Park.

People and the Desert

Deserts are difficult places for people to live. Groups who traditionally live in the desert include the Tuareg of the Sahara, the San of the Kalahari, the Bedouins of the Middle East and North Africa, and the Aboriginal peoples of Australia.

A Tuareg man guides a camel in Algeria's Grand Erg Occidental desert.

Many desert dwellers live in oases. An oasis is a place in the desert with a supply of fresh water. A small number of Bedouin are **nomads**, who migrate into the desert during the rainy season. They move back to other areas in the drier seasons. They also dig wells, grow their own food, and raise animals such as sheep and goats.

In places that are too dry to grow crops, many peoples bring in water from nearby, wetter areas. This is a practice called irrigation. In North African and Asian oases and irrigated areas, some major foods grown include dates, figs, wheat, barley, rice, and beans.

VOCABULARY

Nomads are people who have no permanent home. They move from place to place to find food and water for themselves and their animals.

Oases, like this one in the Libyan desert, provide water and shelter for people and animals.

Irrigation is just one way that humans have changed deserts over time. Some oases once only reached by camel now have airports and gas stations. Some deserts have valuable fossil fuels and minerals that people take out of the ground.

The desert has a balance of life that is easily broken. Too many new things, including new people moving there, can upset that balance.

In other cases the actions of people have turned productive land into new deserts. This process is called

The city of Dubai, in the United Arab Emirates, is in the Arabian Desert.

desertification. It happens when people use the land too much for crops or get rid of too many trees in an area. It also happens because of climate change. Domesticated animals that humans raise for food can also destroy grasslands and other biomes, causing desertification.

Think About It

How might forces like climate change and human population growth affect the deserts we now have ten or twenty years from now?

Fields of palms suffer as the desert spreads in Morocco. Desertification will probably increase as climates change worldwide.

GLOSSARY

burrow To dig a hole in the ground for shelter or protection.

climate change Changes to the world's climates over time, including changes in temperatures, precipitation, and wind patterns.

condense When matter changes from gas into a liquid.

date A fruit that grows on palms in some deserts.

fossil fuels Fuels, such as coal, oil, or natural gas, that formed in the earth from plant or animal remains.

gazelle A small, graceful swift antelope of Africa and Asia.

ibex A type of wild goat.

landform A natural feature of a land surface.

latitudes Areas of Earth measured by lines of latitude, or imaginary lines that circle Earth parallel to the equator.

oryx Any of several long-horned African antelopes.

precipitation Water that falls to the earth from clouds, in the form of rain, snow, sleet, mist, or hail.

sediment Matter that is left behind by water, wind, or glaciers.

shrub a woody plant that has several stems and is smaller than most trees.

species A particular type of living thing.

trait A quality that sets one living thing apart from another.

tundra A treeless plain in the Arctic regions of the world.

For More Information

Books

Gray, Leon. *Deserts*. Tucson, AZ: Brown Bear Books, 2015.

Hollar, Sherman. *Investigating Earth's Desert, Grassland, and Rainforest Biomes*. New York, NY: Britannica Educational Publishing, 2012.

Hunter, Nick. *Deserts*. Chicago, IL: Raintree, 2014.

Kalman, Bobbie. *Where on Earth are Deserts?* St. Catharines, ON: Crabtree Publishing Company, 2014.

Sirvaitis, Karen. *Exploring Deserts*. North Mankato, MN: ABDO Publishing, 2014.

Websites

Kids Do Ecology: World Biomes
http://kids.nceas.ucsb.edu/biomes/desert.html

National Geographic: Desert Information and Facts
https://www.nationalgeographic.com/environment/habitats/deserts
Facebook: @natneo; Twitter: @NatGeo

National Park Service: Science of the American Southwest
https://www.nps.gov/subjects/swscience/deserts.htm
Facebook: @nationalparkservice; Twitter: @NatlParkService

PBS Learning: Desert Biome
https://www.pbslearningmedia.org/resource/tdc02.sci.life.eco.desert/desert-biome
Facebook: @pbslearningmedia; Twitter: @PBSLrnMedia

INDEX